Frida

by Jonah Winter   illustrated by Ana Juan

FRANCES LINCOLN CHILDREN'S BOOKS

For my mother.

— J. W.

To the little artist

who is in your heart.

— A. J.

Frida enters the world.

For little Frida, the world is Mexico.

Her house is a blue house.
It is in the town of Coyoacán.

Frida's father is an artist
and a photographer.

He teaches Frida how to use
a paintbrush.

Frida's mother takes care
of six daughters.
Often she is tired.

Frida is sometimes lonely,
even though she has sisters.

Enter, stage left, Frida's imaginary friend. Her name is Frida too.

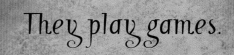
They play games.

All of a sudden, Frida falls very ill. She's in bed for months. There's something wrong with one of her legs. Even her imaginary friend can't cheer her up.

That's when Frida teaches herself how to draw. Drawing saves her from being sad.

When Frida gets better, she carries on with her art. She paints little pictures. They are copies of other paintings.

Painting on to photographs is what Frida's father does for a living. He teaches her how to do this too.

Frida also paints things she sees through a microscope.
She loves looking at things very closely.

At school, Frida studies science.

She is bored. School is too easy.

One day Frida is on the bus home from school.

A horrible accident happens.

A tram crashes into the bus.
Frida almost dies.

In hospital, it is painting that
saves her once again. Painting is
like her imaginary friend.
It is there whenever she wants it.
It keeps her company.
It keeps her from giving up hope.

After the accident, life will never be the same for Frida.
She will walk with a stick – when she is able to walk at all.
Her body will hurt, always.

But Frida doesn't cry or complain. Instead of crying, she paints pictures of herself crying.

When she can't leave her bed, she paints in bed.

When her whole torso is put in a plaster cast, she paints on the cast.

Nothing can stop Frida from painting.
She's often alone, unable to leave her
house, so she has to use her imagination.

She paints what she sees with her eyes –
and on top she paints what she sees
in her heart.
It's almost like painting on photographs.

She paints little magical
scenes with words at the bottom.
All over Mexico, people paint these
kinds of scenes. Sometimes they are
scenes of accidents with angels coming
to the rescue. They are like prayers
for people who are sick. They
are called *exvotos*. Frida
paints *exvotos* of
herself when she is
sick or in pain.

Frida imitates
no one. Her paintings are
like nothing else. In museums,
people still look at them and
weep and sigh and smile.
She turns her pain
into something
beautiful. It is like
a miracle.

AUTHOR'S NOTE

FRIDA KAHLO WAS BORN ON 6th JULY, 1907, in Coyoacán, Mexico, to Guillermo Kahlo and Matilde Calderón de Kahlo. At the age of seven, she was stricken with polio and confined to bed for nine months. The illness left her with a shrunken right leg and a limp. At the age of eighteen, she was in a horrible bus accident that is too nightmarish to describe here.

It's a miracle that she survived and that she was able to produce any art, considering the constant pain she was in throughout the rest of her life. Her paintings are among the most beautiful and original art ever created, and this is a monument to Kahlo's indomitable spirit and willpower. It is proof of her lasting popularity that her paintings continue to be exhibited in museums all over the world and are reproduced in books, on posters and even in advertisements .

Kahlo's popularity began to grow when she married the world-renowned Mexican muralist Diego Rivera in 1929. It has been increasing ever since. Their personalities were both so colourful, and their love for each other so intense, that their marriage remains one of the most famous of the twentieth century.

But it wasn't merely Kahlo's association with the celebrated Rivera that sparked an ongoing public fascination with her. Her painful story is so inspirational that she has become a role model for artists in general, who often must work under difficult conditions. She has specifically been an inspiration to women artists, who have found in Kahlo's strength, courage, and pizzazz an example of how to thrive as a woman in an art world dominated by men.

ARTIST'S NOTE

WORLD-RENOWNED PAINTER FRIDA KAHLO made an important contribution to Mexican art and culture. And in turn, Mexican art and culture played an important part in Frida's development as an artist. For this reason I have portrayed traditional characters in Mexican folk art – funny skeletons, little devils, sweet jaguars and others – as constant companions throughout her life. These are images she would have seen in her childhood home, in the markets of her town and in books. Photographs of the home she shared with Diego Rivera show these characters proudly displayed in the folk art that decorated their rooms.

And as these characters inspired Frida Kahlo, so has Frida Kahlo inspired me. I hope she will inspire you too.

Text copyright © Jonah Winter 2002
Illustrations copyright © Ana Juan 2002

This edition published in 2005 by Frances Lincoln Children's Books,
4 Torriano Mews, Torriano Avenue, London NW5 2RZ

www.franceslincoln.com

First published in the USA by Scholastic Press, New York, USA

British Library Cataloguing in Publication Data available on request

ISBN 1-84507-354-1

Printed in Singapore
1 3 5 7 9 8 6 4 2